Recogn & Eyes

By BriMoral Stories

2

away on a mountain side.

His desire was to create meaningful artwork

My vases!

that would stand
the test of time.

He decided to make

6

cave paintings.

He believed his
artwork would

catch a future
spelunker's eyes.

He fell asleep wondering
what the eventual caver

who discovered his paintings would think.

11

Are you thinking of

what I'm thinking of?

of you!

I'm thinking about how

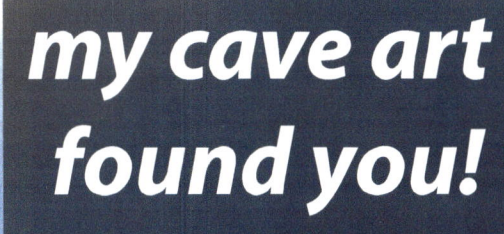

I hope
you feel

the same fortune too.

We can see

eye to eye.

www.ingramcontent.com/pod-product-compliance
Lightning Source LLC
Chambersburg PA
CBHW041010170626
46815CB00002B/238